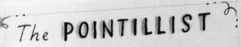

The POINTILLIST

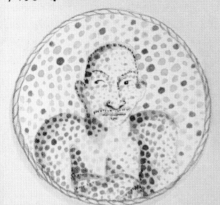

COUNTRY of ORIGIN... FRANCE
RECORD... 22 WINS, 4 LOSSES
ATTRIBUTES... PINPOINT ACCURACY,
DISAPPEARS UP CLOSE, CONFUSES THE
COLOR-BLIND

The ANACONDA

COUNTRY of ORIGIN... BRAZIL
RECORD... 36 WINS, 1 LOSS
ATTRIBUTES... BULGING MUSCLES,
SQUEEZING ABILITY, SLIPPERY SKIN

The MISANTHROPE

COUNTRY of ORIGIN... FRANCE
RECORD... 3 WINS, 3 LOSSES
ATTRIBUTES... SURLINESS, DISDAIN
for OPPONENT, CAUSTIC WIT

The AFRICAN CHEF

COUNTRY of ORIGIN... CHAD
RECORD... 79 WINS, 1 LOSS
ATTRIBUTES... BLINDING PATE,
HAIRLESS BODY, USE of KITCHEN TOOLS

LALOUCHE

COUNTRY of ORIGIN... FRANCE
RECORD... UNDEFEATED!
ATTRIBUTES... BLAZING SPEED,
MAGNIFICENT MUSTACHE, ESCAPE SKILLS

AMPÈRE

COUNTRY of ORIGIN... FRANCE
RECORD... 15 WINS, 2 LOSSES
ATTRIBUTES... SHOCK TACTICS, USE
of STUN HOLDS, CAN GALVANIZE a CROWD

For S.B. —M.O.
For M.O. —S.B.

GLOSSARY

C'est impossible—It's impossible

Défense d'afficher—Post no bills

Je suis désolé—I'm sorry

Pardon, monsieur—Excuse me, sir

S'il vous plaît—Please

Voilà—There you have it

SCHWARTZ & WADE BOOKS

THE MIGHTY LALOUCHE

written by Matthew Olshan
illustrated by Sophie Blackall

One hundred and a few–odd years ago,
in Paris, France, there lived
a humble postman named Lalouche.
He was small, Lalouche,
and rather bony,

but his hands
were nimble,

his legs were fast,

and his arms were strong.

For company, he kept a finch
named Geneviève.
His mustache was his other pride and joy.
Lalouche's rented room was on the Seine,
but, unlike all the other rented rooms,
it lacked a window with a view.
Lalouche pretended not to mind,
but how he wished to see
the brand-new city lights!

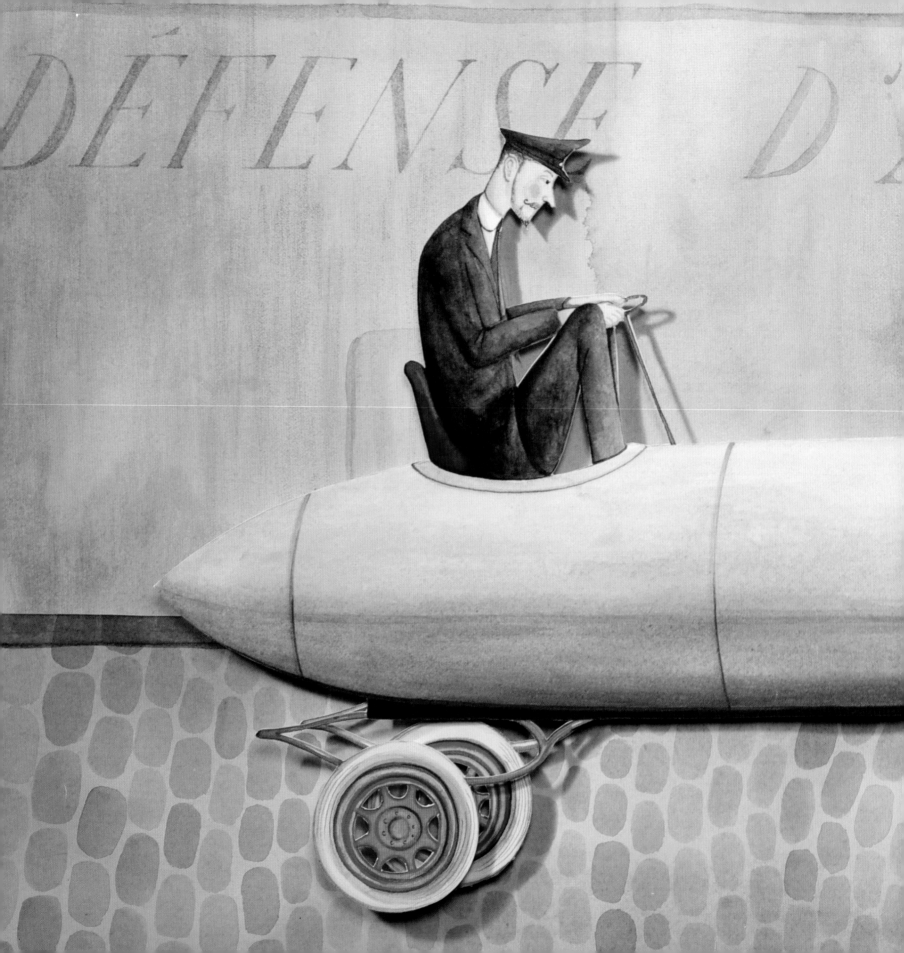

One day, Lalouche's boss pulled up and said,
"Look here, Lalouche. The postal service
has just bought a fleet of electric autocars.
A walking postman's far too slow.
Je suis désolé, but we're going to have to let you go."

And just like that, Lalouche was sacked.

Without a job, he'd lose his rented room.
Without a room, there'd be no place for Geneviève.

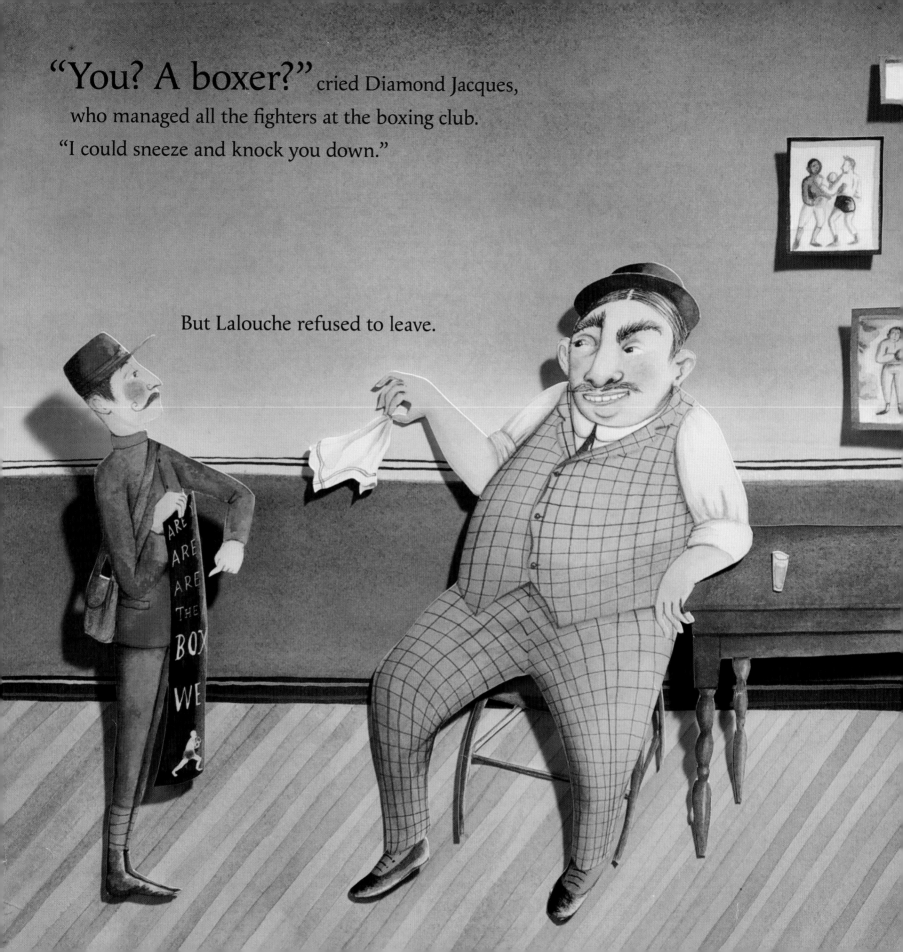

"You? A boxer?" cried Diamond Jacques, who managed all the fighters at the boxing club. "I could sneeze and knock you down."

But Lalouche refused to leave.

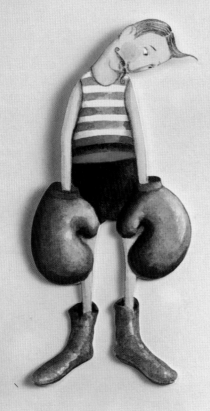

Grown-up gloves and boxing booties
were much too big.

Luckily, the school next door
had spares.

The boxers all laughed when they saw Lalouche.

"I'll zap him!"
cried Ampère.

"I'll pound
him to a pulp,"
said the Piston.

"But first,
I'll tie him in
a pretty bow,"
said the Grecque.

"What do I do?" asked Lalouche, in the ring at last.

"Hit me,"
said the Grecque.

"C'est impossible,"
said Lalouche.

"Suit yourself!" the Grecque replied.
He was a master wrestler who liked
to twist opponents into pretzels . . .

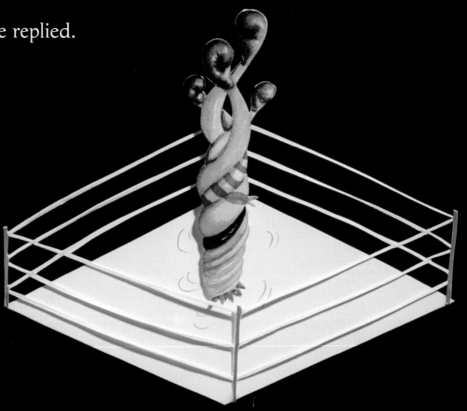

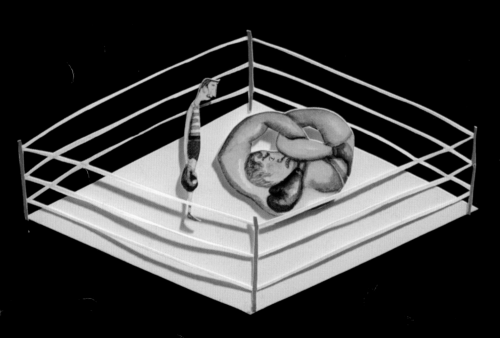

but Lalouche was just too nimble.

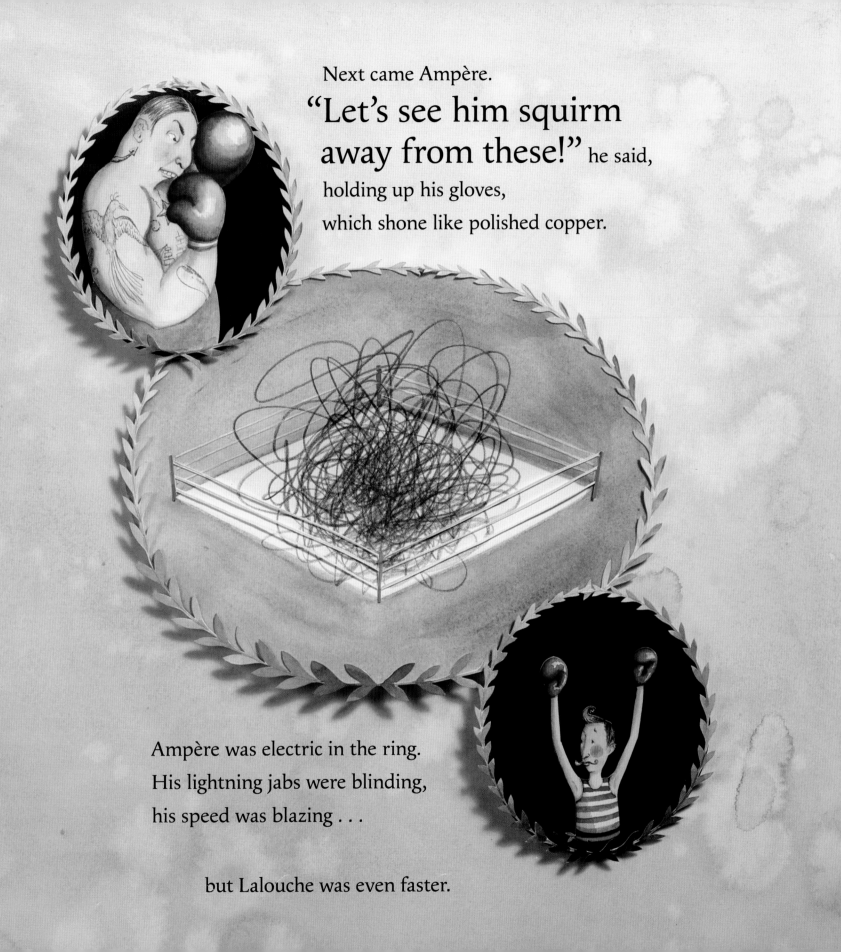

Next came Ampère.

"Let's see him squirm away from these!" he said,
holding up his gloves,
which shone like polished copper.

Ampère was electric in the ring.
His lightning jabs were blinding,
his speed was blazing . . .

but Lalouche was even faster.

"Enough of this tomfoolery," the Piston said.

"It's time to crush the little man."

The Piston leaped high into the air and landed on Lalouche.

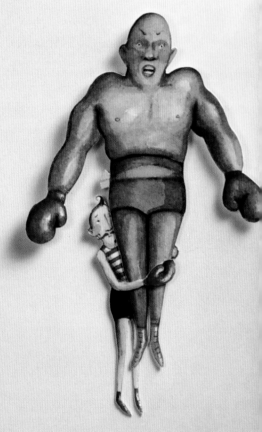

The postman crumpled to the mat.

"Voilà!" the Piston cried.

"It just takes strength."

But Lalouche was even stronger.

"What's happening?" the Piston groaned.

"Pardon, monsieur," said Lalouche.

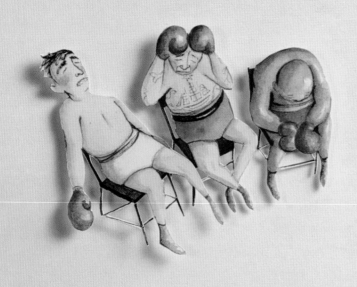

"I hope I didn't hurt them," said Lalouche.
"Forget all that," said Diamond Jacques.
"You're a sensation!
  Next Friday night, you'll fight the Anaconda,
  the biggest, baddest beast
  this city's ever seen."
"Will I have to hit him?" asked Lalouche.
"Only if you want to live!"
  said Diamond Jacques.

The harness muscleman was huge,
as tall as a spiral staircase,
as wide as a wall of cubbies,
as massive as a heap of undelivered packages.
Lalouche struck a gallant fighting pose.

"I'll squeeze him till he pops!"
the Anaconda roared.

The bell rang out. The fight began.

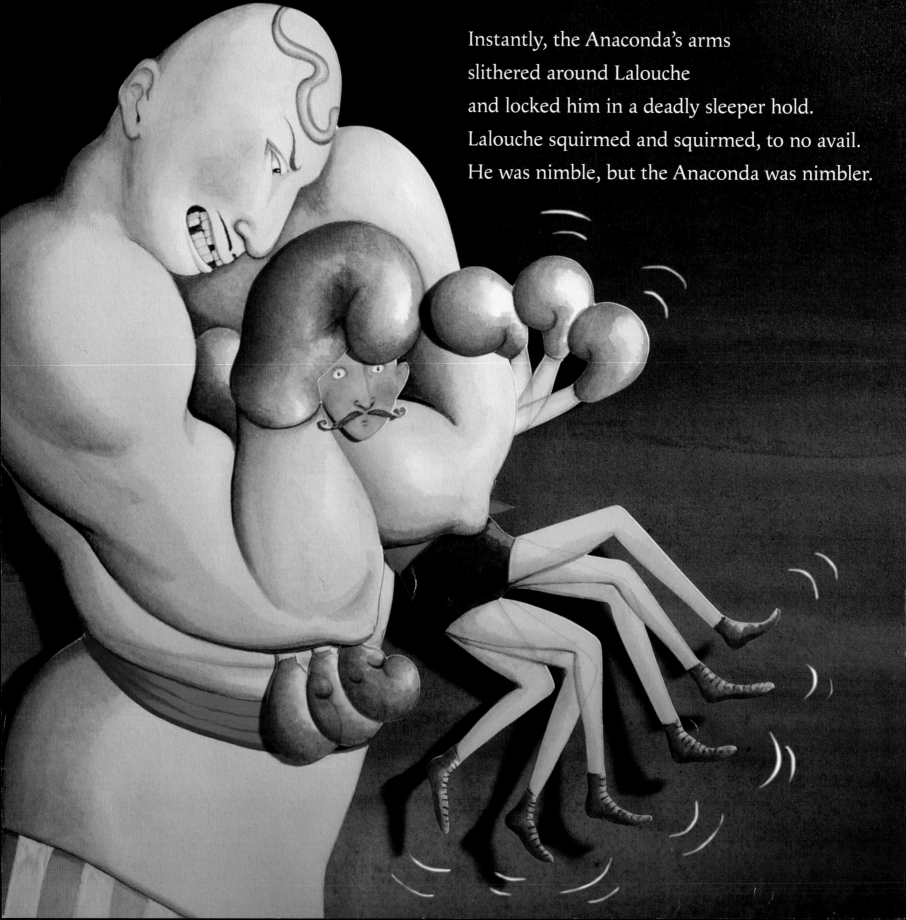

Instantly, the Anaconda's arms
slithered around Lalouche
and locked him in a deadly sleeper hold.
Lalouche squirmed and squirmed, to no avail.
He was nimble, but the Anaconda was nimbler.

Just then, the first round ended.

Lucky for Lalouche!

"Don't give up," said Diamond Jacques.

"Confuse him with your speed."

Lalouche's booties skipped across the canvas.

He feinted left, then right.

His punches were too fast to see,

his gloves a whistling blur.

He ran figure eights around the Anaconda's legs.

He was fast, but the Anaconda was faster.

Round three began.

With one enormous stride,

the Anaconda stomped Lalouche.

The little fighter was pinned.

He was strong, but the Anaconda was stronger.

The Anaconda knew he'd won.

He grinned and took a moment to impress the crowd

by kneeling down and flexing his gigantic gleaming arms.

But one should never underestimate a man who loves his finch. Lalouche sprang up.

"For country, mail, and Geneviève!" he cried.

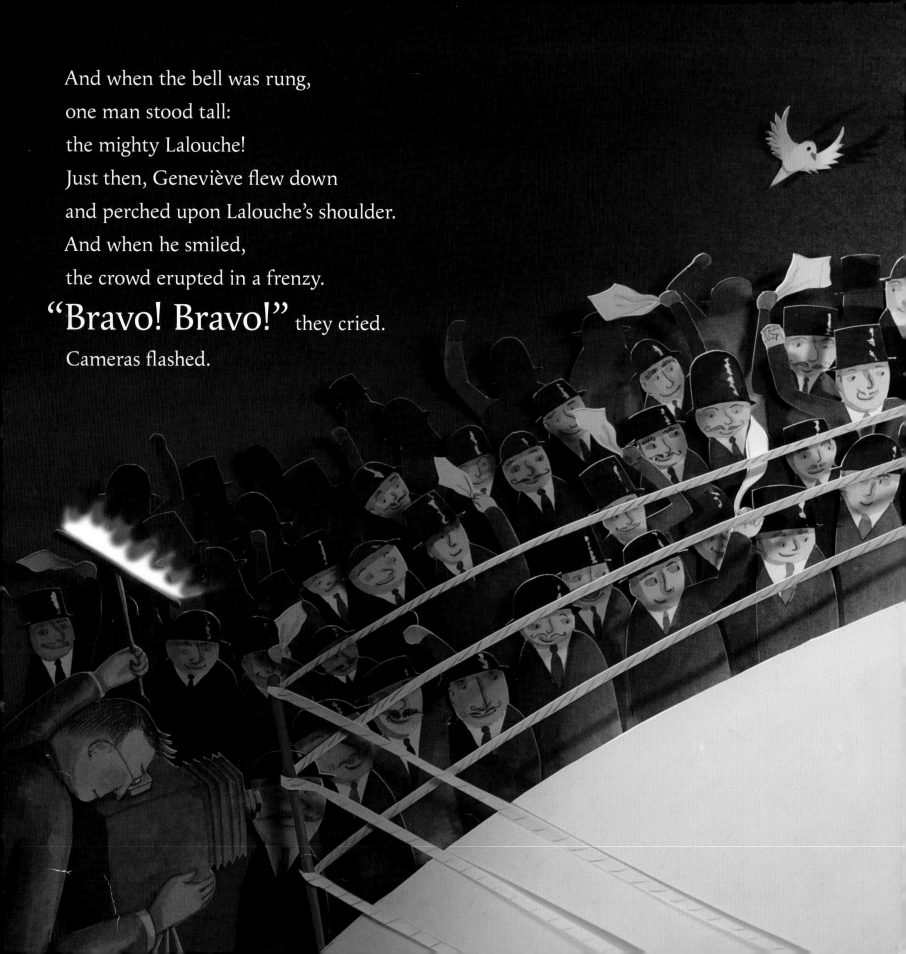

And when the bell was rung,

one man stood tall:

the mighty Lalouche!

Just then, Geneviève flew down

and perched upon Lalouche's shoulder.

And when he smiled,

the crowd erupted in a frenzy.

"Bravo! Bravo!" they cried.

Cameras flashed.

From that day on, Lalouche fought every challenger
who dared to climb into the ring—
Old Shatterhand and Blériot;
the Bolshevik, the Pointillist, and even the Misanthrope.
He never lost. They never won.

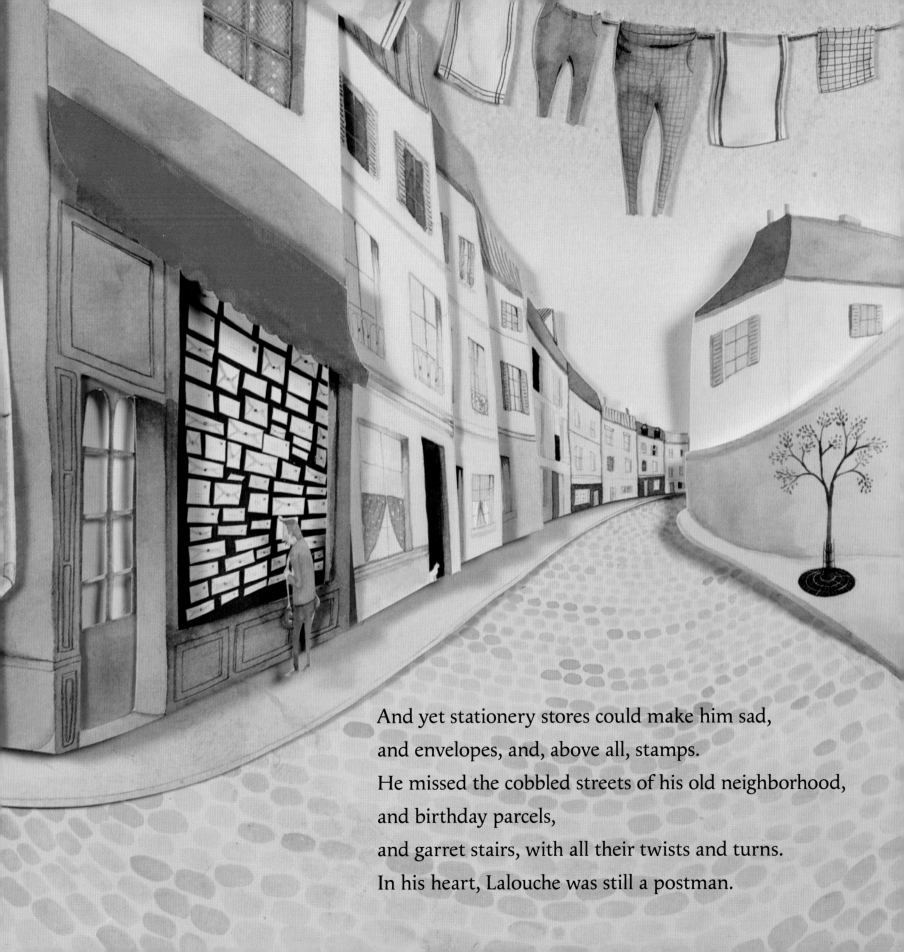

And yet stationery stores could make him sad,
and envelopes, and, above all, stamps.
He missed the cobbled streets of his old neighborhood,
and birthday parcels,
and garret stairs, with all their twists and turns.
In his heart, Lalouche was still a postman.

So when his old boss called and said,
"These autocars have been a complete disaster.
S'il vous plaît, would you consider your old job?"
Lalouche's boxing days were done.

"You can't retire," cried Diamond Jacques.
"The people need you!"
"Perhaps," Lalouche replied,
"but even more, the people need their mail."

And just like that, Lalouche traded
in his famous gloves and booties
for a humble postman's uniform.
He reported to his old post office
at the crack of dawn, and in no time,
people had forgotten
he'd ever been gone.
All was just as it had been.
With one exception . . .

At the end of a long day,
after all the mail was finally delivered
and the sorting room was tidied up and swept,
Lalouche would stretch, and yawn, and head back home
to Geneviève, and to his old apartment building on the Seine,
where he'd taken a new room
with skylights and a special nook for Geneviève,
and a most spectacular view.

❧ AUTHOR'S NOTE ❧

La boxe française, or French boxing, was a popular sport in Paris in the late nineteenth century. While boxing in England and America allowed only punching, in French boxing, fighters could use their feet as well as their fists. The result was a sport that looked a lot like today's kickboxing.

La boxe française favored speed and agility over brute strength. In other words, a quick and nimble boxer like Lalouche would have stood a decent chance of winning against bigger and stronger opponents. The matches weren't free-for-alls, though. Some of the moves the fighters use in this story—like the Piston's stomping or the Anaconda's slithery sleeper hold—wouldn't have been strictly legal.

In the late 1890s and early 1900s, the French public was captivated by advancements in the electric car. Early gasoline-powered cars were noisy, stinky, and unreliable; electric cars, on the other hand, were quiet, smokeless, and easier to drive.

In reading about the Paris my little postman would have known, I came across a photograph of a man crammed into what looked like a rocket on wheels. It turned out to be a famous electric race car, *La Jamais Contente,* which means "The Never Satisfied." I sent the picture to Sophie Blackall, who decided to work it into her illustrations.

Of course, *La Jamais Contente* was built for speed, not for cargo. It's unlikely the French postal service would have chosen a race car to help deliver the mail. But can't you just picture a whole fleet of them . . . gone wrong?

Visit us on the Web! randomhouse.com/kids
Educators and librarians, for a variety of teaching tools, visit us at RHTeachersLibrarians.com

Library of Congress Cataloging-in-Publication Data
Olshan, Matthew.
The Mighty Lalouche / Matthew Olshan ; illustrated by Sophie Blackall.—1st ed.
p. cm.
Summary: In Paris, France, more than a hundred years ago, a small man named Lalouche is let go
from his job as a mail carrier and discovers that he has great skill as a fighter.
ISBN 978-0-375-86225-0 (trade)
ISBN 978-0-375-96225-7 (glb)
[1. Boxing—Fiction. 2. Letter carriers—Fiction.
3. Paris (France)—History—20th century—Fiction.
4. France—History—Third Republic, 1870–1940—Fiction.] I. Blackall, Sophie, ill. II. Title.
PZ7.O51788Mig 2012
[E]—dc22
2010031825

The text of this book is set in Apolline.
The illustrations in this book were made with Chinese ink and watercolor on
Arches hot press paper. They were cut out, arranged in layers, and photographed.
Book design by Rachael Cole

MANUFACTURED IN CHINA
10 9 8 7 6 5 4 3 2 1
First Edition

Random House Children's Books supports the First Amendment and celebrates the right to read.

The FERRYMAN

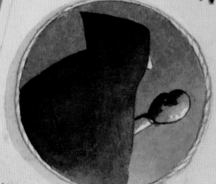

COUNTRY of ORIGIN... ROMANIA
RECORD... 12 WINS, 1 DRAW, 1 LOSS
ATTRIBUTES... INDIFFERENT, GRIM,
OFTEN OBSCURED BY BLACK CLOAK

BLÉRIOT

COUNTRY of ORIGIN... FRANCE
RECORD... 64 WINS, 1 LOSS
ATTRIBUTES... LIGHTER THAN AIR,
SUPERB GROOMING, UNAFRAID of HEIGHTS

The GRECQUE

COUNTRY of ORIGIN... GREECE
RECORD... 23 WINS, 1 LOSS
ATTRIBUTES... PERFECT TEETH,
UNBLEMISHED GOOD LOOKS, SNEAKINESS

The BOLSHEVIK

COUNTRY of ORIGIN... RUSSIA
RECORD... CLASSIFIED
ATTRIBUTES... IMPERVIOUS TO COLD,
CAN SURVIVE ON FISH EGGS, FIERY TEMPER

OLD SHATTERHAND

COUNTRY of ORIGIN... GERMANY
RECORD... 124 WINS, 1 LOSS
ATTRIBUTES... DRESSES LIKE A COWBOY,
THINKS HE IS A COWBOY, KNOWS ROPE TRICKS

The PISTON

COUNTRY of ORIGIN... U.S.A.
RECORD... 29 WINS, 1 LOSS
ATTRIBUTES... RAMROD POSTURE,
EXPLOSIVE PUNCH, OFTEN QUITE OILY